W9-CEP-835

EDGAR ALLAN POE
THE SELECTED WORKS

EDGAR ALLAN POE
The Selected Works

RUNNING PRESS
PHILADELPHIA · LONDON

A Running Press® Miniature Edition™
© 2014 by Running Press

Printed in China

9 8 7 6 5

Digit on the right indicates the number of
this printing

Library of Congress Control Number: 2014935538

ISBN 978-0-7624-5492-1

Running Press Book Publishers
A Member of the Perseus Books Group
2300 Chestnut Street
Philadelphia, PA 19103-4371

Visit us on the web!
www.runningpress.com

CONTENTS

TALES

INTRODUCTION

As an American literary icon, Edgar Allan Poe as a person is often shrouded in the same macabre light as that of his writings. Legends paint him as a madman, haunted by inner demons and vices—and his work a mere reflection of his insanity.

But underneath that fabrication is a person who was raised a gentleman and who crafted masterpieces of incredible imaginings. What cannot be denied, though, is that the atmosphere of his life was ripe with grief and isolation, accompanied by the loss of loved ones and professional strife as he struggled to make a living with his creative pursuits.

And that troubled tone echoes in his writings. We easily label Poe now as an editor, critic, poet, and short-story writer, but they are titles that he struggled through poverty to earn over time.

In this collection, we celebrate the "master of suspense" with six selected poems and four short stories that are full of mystery and horror. The poems include *The Raven*, *To Helen*, *The City in the Sea*, *A Dream Within a Dream*, *The Conqueror Worm*, and *The Bells*. First published anonymously in the *New York Evening Mirror* in 1845, *The Raven* has grown to become one of the most famous poems in literary history. *To Helen* was first printed in *Poems* in 1831, and some say it is about Jane

Stith Craig Stanard, who Poe knew from Richmond growing up. *The City in the Sea*, possibly about the cities of Sodom and Gomorrah (beneath the Dead Sea), also first appeared in *Poems* in 1831. In *A Dream Within a Dream* (1849) Poe reflects on a philosophical topic that has been pondered for thousands of years. *The Conqueror Worm*, first published by Graham's

Magazine in January 1843, transports you into a play. And the last major poem of Poe's life, put in print by *Home Journal* in 1849, was *The Bells*.

The four haunting short stories included in this collection are *The Masque of the Red Death* (1842), *The Tell-Tale Heart* (1843), *The Cask of Amontillado* (1847), and *The Black Cat* (1843). Out of all of the stories Poe wrote, *The Tell-Tale Heart* is arguably known as the most terrifying. His tales have captivated readers across the ages and the way he crafted them with thrill and intrigue has garnered him the title "the father of detective stories." The door into his chill-inducing, mysterious world awaits you.

THE LIFE OF EDGAR ALLAN POE

Edgar Allan Poe was born in Boston, Massachusetts on January 19, 1809 to two actors, Elizabeth Arnold Hopkins and David Poe, Jr. He had an older brother, William

Poe's home, Philadelphia

Leonard Poe, and a younger sister, Rosalie Poe. The former became a poet and died young of tuberculosis and the latter grew up to become a teacher at a girls' school. Their family dispersed when Edgar's mother died from tuberculosis when he was two years old. Prior, his father disappeared.

Elizabeth, Poe's mother

Edgar was taken into the family of John and Frances Valentine Allan, who lived in Richmond, Virginia. As a tobacco merchant, John Allan provided for Edgar and attempted to raise him as a businessman. But the desire of young Edgar's heart always harkened to poetry, wanting to be like British poet Lord Byron. By age thirteen he had started to answer that calling, despite the differences between himself and John Allan.

In 1826, Allan supported Poe while he attended the University of Virginia to study Latin and French, but only for one term, whereupon Poe took up gambling to try to pay off

debts. He was forced to
return home, where further
heartbreak awaited him—
his fiancée Sarah Elmira
Royster had been prom-
ised to another man in his
absence.

The following year, Poe
began a short-lived mil-
itary career and enlisted
into the army as Edgar A.
Perry. That same year, at the

age of eighteen, he culti-
vated his first collection of
poetry, *Tamerlane and Other
Poems*, and got it published.
After two years as a private
soldier, he experienced
another loss in his life—
the death of his adopted
mother, Frances Valentine
Allan, to tuberculosis.

At twenty-one, with
the help of John Allan,

Poe entered the Military Academy at West Point, but he only spent eight months there. He intentionally got himself thrown out, in order to pursue his literary passion. And he did—he published his third collection simply titled *Poems* in the aftermath.

For a brief period afterwards, he called Baltimore,

Maryland, his home and lived with his aunt, Maria Clemm, and his cousin, Virginia (who at thirteen married him); they cohabitated with his grandmother (Elizabeth Poe) and his brother. When John Allan passed away in 1834, he left Edgar nothing. So for the rest of his life Poe struggled financially and moved a lot to find work.

Although we commonly associate Poe with being a writer of his own original imaginings, he made his living mainly by criticizing others'. He was known as a "fearless critic" for his brash reviews, which started at the *Southern Literary Messenger* in Richmond. Between 1835 and 1845, Poe tried to fight poverty by moving from

Virginia to New York City
to Philadelphia and back
to New York in order to
find magazine work, while
attempting to write novels
and poetry on the side.

While living in Phila-
delphia in 1839, his first
book of short stories *Tales
of the Grotesque and Arabesque*
was published by Lea &
Blanchard. But it wasn't

until 1845, when *The Raven and Other Poems* (Wiley & Putnam, New York) entered the literary world that Poe's name began to draw attention. Not only did people gather for his lectures, but he had also gained the credibility to ask for more money for his work.

As one aspect of his life came together, though,

another fell apart. In 1942, tuberculosis struck his wife Virginia, like so many others in his past, and in 1847 she died at age twenty-four. In those five years, Poe turned to alcohol to ease his devastation. In the two years that followed Virginia's death, Poe reconnected with and engaged Elmira Royster Shelton (who was widowed) in Richmond. He traveled to lecture and find people to support his proposed magazine endeavor, *The Stylus*.

Much mystery surrounds Poe's death in 1849. On a trip from Richmond to Philadelphia, he briefly stopped in Baltimore, where his whereabouts went unknown for days.

He was found in a bar on October 3 and passed away at Washington College Hospital in a coma, on October 7. His body resides now next to his wife Virginia's in Baltimore, where his legacy lives on in not only his literary masterpieces but also the city itself.

POEMS

THE RAVEN

Once upon a mid-
night dreary, while I pondered, weak and weary,
Over many a quaint and curious
volume of forgotten lore,
While I nodded, nearly napping,
suddenly there came a tapping,
As of some one gently rapping,
rapping at my chamber door.

"'Tis some visitor," I muttered,
  "tapping at my chamber door—
Only this, and nothing more."

Ah, distinctly I remember it was
  in the bleak December,
And each separate dying ember
  wrought its ghost upon the
  floor.
Eagerly I wished the morrow;
  vainly I had sought to borrow
From my books surcease of
  sorrow—sorrow for the lost

Lenore—
For the rare and radiant maiden
  whom the angels name
Lenore—
Nameless here for evermore.

And the silken sad uncertain
  rustling of each purple curtain
Thrilled me—filled me with
  fantastic terrors never felt
  before;
So that now, to still the beating
  of my heart, I stood repeating

"'Tis some visitor entreating
  entrance at my chamber door—
Some late visitor entreating
  entrance at my chamber door;—
This it is, and nothing more."

Presently my soul grew stronger;
  hesitating then no longer,
"Sir," said I, "or Madam, truly
  your forgiveness I implore;
But the fact is I was napping,
  and so gently you came rapping,
And so faintly you came tapping,

tapping at my chamber door,
That I scarce was sure I heard
  you"—here I opened wide the
  door;—
Darkness there and nothing more.

Deep into that darkness peering,
  long I stood there wondering,
  fearing,
Doubting, dreaming dreams no
  mortal ever dared to dream
  before;
But the silence was unbroken,

and the darkness gave no token,
And the only word there spoken
  was the whispered word,
"Lenore!"
This I whispered, and an echo
murmured back the word,
"Lenore!"—
Merely this, and nothing more.

Back into the chamber turning,
all my soul within me burning,
Soon again I heard a tapping
somewhat louder than before.

"Surely," said I, "surely that is
something at my window lattice;
Let me see, then, what threat is,
and this mystery explore—
Let my heart be still a moment
and this mystery explore;—
'Tis the wind and nothing
more!"

Open here I flung the shutter, when,
with many a flirt and flutter,
In there stepped a stately raven
of the saintly days of yore;

Not the least obeisance made he;
  not an instant stopped or stayed
  he;
But, with mien of lord or lady,
  perched above my chamber
  door—
Perched upon a bust of Pallas
  just above my chamber door—
Perched, and sat, and nothing
  more.

Then this ebony bird beguiling
  my sad fancy into smiling,

By the grave and stern decorum
   of the countenance it wore,
"Though thy crest be shorn and
   shaven, thou," I said, "art sure
   no craven,
Ghastly grim and ancient raven
   wandering from the Nightly
   shore—
Tell me what thy lordly name is
   on the Night's Plutonian
   shore!"
Quoth the raven "Nevermore."

Much I marvelled this ungainly
  fowl to hear discourse so plainly,
Though its answer little
  meaning—little relevancy bore;
For we cannot help agreeing that
  no living human being
Ever yet was blessed with seeing
  bird above his chamber door—
Bird or beast upon the sculptured
  bust above his chamber door,
With such name as "Nevermore."

But the raven, sitting lonely on

44

the placid bust, spoke only
That one word, as if his soul in
that one word he did outpour.
Nothing farther then he uttered
not a feather then he fluttered—
Till I scarcely more than
muttered "Other friends have
flown before—
On the morrow he will leave
me, as my hopes have flown
before."
Then the bird said "Nevermore."

Startled at the stillness broken by
  reply so aptly spoken,
"Doubtless," said I, "what it
  utters is its only stock and store
Caught from some unhappy
  master whom unmerciful
Disaster
Followed fast and followed faster
  till his songs one burden bore—
Till the dirges of his Hope that
  melancholy burden bore
Of 'Never—nevermore.'"

But the raven still beguiling all
  my sad soul into smiling,
Straight I wheeled a cushioned
  seat in front of bird, and bust
  and door;
Then, upon the velvet sinking, I
  betook myself to linking
Fancy unto fancy, thinking what
  this ominous bird of yore—
What this grim, ungainly,
  ghastly, gaunt and ominous
  bird of yore

Meant in croaking "Nevermore."

This I sat engaged in guessing,
  but no syllable expressing
To the fowl whose fiery eyes now
  burned into my bosom's core;
This and more I sat divining,
  with my head at ease reclining
On the cushion's velvet lining
  that the lamplight gloated o'er,
But whose velvet violet lining
  with the lamplight gloating o'er,
She shall press, ah, nevermore!

Then, methought, the air grew
    denser, perfumed from an
    unseen censer
Swung by Angels whose faint
    foot-falls tinkled on the tufted
    floor.
"Wretch," I cried, "thy God hath
    lent thee—by these angels he
    hath sent thee
Respite—respite and nepenthe
    from thy memories of Lenore;
Quaff, oh quaff this kind nepenthe

and forget this lost Lenore!"
Quoth the raven, "Nevermore."

"Prophet!" said I, "thing of evil!
  prophet still, if bird or devil!—
Whether Tempter sent, or
  whether tempest tossed thee
  here ashore,
Desolate yet all undaunted, on
  this desert land enchanted—
On this home by Horror
  haunted—tell me truly, I
  implore—

Is there—is there balm in
  Gilead?—tell me—tell me,
  I implore!"
Quoth the raven, "Nevermore."

"Prophet!" said I, "thing of evil
  prophet still, if bird or devil!
By that Heaven that bends above
  us—by that God we both adore—
Tell this soul with sorrow laden
  if, within the distant Aidenn,
It shall clasp a sainted maiden
  whom the angels name

Lenore—
Clasp a rare and radiant maiden
    whom the angels name Lenore."
Quoth the raven, "Nevermore."

"Be that word our sign of
    parting, bird or fiend!" I
    shrieked, upstarting—
"Get thee back into the tempest
    and the Night's Plutonian
    shore!
Leave no black plume as a token
    of that lie thy soul hath spoken!

Leave my loneliness unbroken!
  quit the bust above my door!
Take thy beak from out my
  heart, and take thy form from
  off my door!"
Quoth the raven, "Nevermore."

And the raven, never flitting, still
  is sitting, still is sitting
On the pallid bust of Pallas just
  above my chamber door;
And his eyes have all the seeming
  of a demon's that is dreaming,

And the lamp-light o'er him
  streaming throws his shadow
  on the floor;
And my soul from out that
  shadow that lies floating on
  the floor
Shall be lifted—nevermore!

TO HELEN

Helen, thy beauty
is to me
Like those Nicéan
 barks of yore,
That gently, o'er a perfumed sea,
The weary, way-worn wanderer
 bore
To his own native shore.

On desperate seas long wont to
  roam,
Thy hyacinth hair, thy classic
  face,
Thy Naiad airs have brought me
  home
To the glory that was Greece,
And the grandeur that was
  Rome.

Lo! in yon brilliant
  window-niche

How statue-like I see thee stand,
The agate lamp within thy
  hand!
Ah, Psyche, from the regions
  which
Are Holy-Land!

THE CITY
IN THE SEA

Lo! Death has reared
himself a throne
In a strange city lying
alone
Far down within the dim West,
Where the good and the bad and
the worst and the best
Have gone to their eternal rest.

There shrines and palaces and
  towers
(Time-eaten towers that tremble
  not!)
Resemble nothing that is ours.
Around, by lifting winds forgot,
Resignedly beneath the sky
The melancholy waters lie.

No rays from the holy heaven
  come down
On the long night-time of that
  town;

But light from out the lurid sea
Streams up the turrets silently—
Gleams up the pinnacles far and
  free—
Up domes—up spires—up
  kingly halls—
Up fanes—up Babylon-like
  walls—
Up shadowy long-forgotten
  bowers
Of sculptured ivy and stone
  flowers—

Up many and many a
  marvellous shrine
Whose wreathéd friezes
  intertwine
The viol, the violet, and the vine.
Resignedly beneath the sky
The melancholy waters lie.
So blend the turrets and shadows
  there
That all seem pendulous in air,
While from a proud tower in the
  town

Death looks gigantically down.
There open fanes and gaping
  graves
Yawn level with the luminous
  waves;
But not the riches there that lie
In each idol's diamond eye—

Not the gaily-jewelled dead
Tempt the waters from their bed;
For no ripples curl, alas!
Along that wilderness of glass—

No swellings tell that winds
   may be
Upon some far-off happier sea—
No heavings hint that winds
   have been
On seas less hideously serene.

But lo, a stir is in the air!
The wave—there is a movement
   here!
As if the towers had thrown
   aside,

In slightly sinking, the dull
   tide—
As if their tops had feebly given
A void within the filmy Heaven.
The waves have now a redder
   glow—
The hours are breathing faint
   and low—
And when, amid no earthly
   moans,
Down, down that town shall
   settle hence,

Hell, rising from a thousand
  thrones,
Shall do it reverence.

A DREAM
WITHIN A
DREAM

Take this kiss upon
the brow!
And, in parting from
you now,
Thus much let me avow—
You are not wrong, who deem

That my days have been a
  dream;
Yet if hope has flown away
In a night, or in a day,
In a vision, or in none,
Is it therefore the less gone?
All that we see or seem
Is but a dream within a dream.

I stand amid the roar
Of a surf-tormented shore,
And I hold within my hand
Grains of the golden sand—

How few! yet how they creep
Through my fingers to the deep,
While I weep—while I weep!
O God! can I not grasp
Them with a tighter clasp?
O God! can I not save
One from the pitiless wave?
Is all that we see or seem
But a dream within a dream?

THE CONQUEROR WORM

Lo! 'tis a gala night
Within the lonesome
latter years!
An angel throng, bewinged, bedight
In veils, and drowned in tears,
Sit in a theatre, to see

A play of hopes and fears,
While the orchestra breathes
 fitfully
The music of the spheres.

Mimes, in the form of God on
 high,
Mutter and mumble low,
And hither and thither fly—
Mere puppets they, who come
 and go
At bidding of vast formless things
That shift the scenery to and fro,

70

Flapping from out their Condor
  wings
Invisible Woe!

That motley drama—oh, be sure
It shall not be forgot!
With its Phantom chased for
  evermore,
By a crowd that seize it not,
Through a circle that ever
  returneth in
To the self-same spot,
And much of Madness, and
  more of Sin,

And Horror the soul of the plot.

But see, amid the mimic rout
A crawling shape intrude!
A blood-red thing that writhes
from out
The scenic solitude!
It writhes!—it writhes!—with
mortal pangs
The mimes become its food,
And the angels sob at vermin
fangs
In human gore imbued.

Out—out are the lights—out all!
And, over each quivering form,
The curtain, a funeral pall,
Comes down with the rush of a
  storm,
And the angels, all pallid and
  wan,
Uprising, unveiling, affirm
That the play is the tragedy,
"Man,"
And its hero the Conqueror Worm.

THE BELLS

I.

Hear the sledges with the bells—

Silver bells!

*What a world of merriment their
melody foretells!*

How they tinkle, tinkle, tinkle,

In the icy air of night!

While the stars that oversprinkle

All the heavens, seem to twinkle

With a crystalline delight;

Keeping time, time, time,
In a sort of Runic rhyme,
To the tintinnabulation that so
  musically wells
From the bells, bells, bells, bells,
Bells, bells, bells—
From the jingling and the tin-
kling of the bells.

II.

Hear the mellow wedding
  bells

Golden bells!

What a world of happiness their
  harmony foretells!
Through the balmy air of night
How they ring out their
  delight!—
From the molten-golden notes,
And all in tune,
What a liquid ditty floats
To the turtle-dove that listens,
  while she gloats
On the moon!
Oh, from out the sounding cells,

What a gush of euphony
  voluminously wells!
How it swells!
How it dwells
On the Future!—how it tells
Of the rapture that impels
To the swinging and the ringing
Of the bells, bells, bells—
Of the bells, bells, bells, bells,
Bells, bells, bells—
To the rhyming and the chiming
  of the bells!

III.
Hear the loud alarum bells—
Brazen bells!
What tale of terror, now their
  turbulency tells!
In the startled ear of night
How they scream out their
  affright!
Too much horrified to speak,
They can only shriek, shriek,
Out of tune,
In a clamorous appealing to the
  mercy of the fire,

In a mad expostulation with the
   deaf and frantic fire,
Leaping higher, higher, higher,
With a desperate desire,
And a resolute endeavor
Now—now to sit, or never,
By the side of the pale-faced
   moon.
Oh, the bells, bells, bells!
What a tale their terror tells
Of Despair!
How they clang, and clash, and
   roar!

What a horror they outpour
On the bosom of the palpitating
   air!
Yet the ear, it fully knows,
By the twanging
And the clanging,
How the danger ebbs and flows;
Yet the ear distinctly tells,
In the jangling,
And the wrangling,
How the danger sinks and
   swells,

By the sinking or the swelling in
  the anger of the bells—
Of the bells—
Of the bells, bells, bells, bells,
Bells, bells, bells—
In the clamor and the clanging
  of the bells!

IV.

Hear the tolling of the bells—

Iron bells!

What a world of solemn thought
  their monody compels!

In the silence of the night,

How we shiver with affright

At the melancholy menace of
  their tone!

For every sound that floats

From the rust within their
  throats

Is a groan.
And the people—ah, the people—
They that dwell up in the steeple,
All alone,
And who, tolling, tolling,
  tolling,
In that muffled monotone,
Feel a glory in so rolling
On the human heart a stone—
They are neither man nor
  woman—

They are neither brute nor
  human—
They are Ghouls:—
And their king it is who tolls:—
And he rolls, rolls, rolls,
Rolls
A pæan from the bells!
And his merry bosom swells
With the pæan of the bells!
And he dances, and he yells;
Keeping time, time, time,
In a sort of Runic rhyme,

To the pæan of the bells:—
Of the bells:
Keeping time, time, time,
In a sort of Runic rhyme,
To the throbbing of the bells—
Of the bells, bells, bells—
To the sobbing of the bells:—
Keeping time, time, time,
As he knells, knells, knells,
In a happy Runic rhyme,
To the rolling of the bells—
Of the bells, bells, bells:—

To the tolling of the bells—
Of the bells, bells, bells, bells,
Bells, bells, bells—
To the moaning and the
  groaning of the bells.

TALES

THE MASQUE
OF THE
RED DEATH

The "Red Death" had long devastated the country. No pestilence had ever been so fatal, or so hideous. Blood was its Avatar and its seal—the redness and the horror of blood. There were sharp pains,

and sudden dizziness, and
then profuse bleeding at
the pores, with dissolution.
The scarlet stains upon the
body and especially upon
the face of the victim, were
the pest ban which shut
him out from the aid and
from the sympathy of his
fellow-men. And the whole
seizure, progress, and
termination of the disease,

were the incidents of half
an hour.

But the Prince Prospero
was happy and daunt-
less and sagacious. When
his dominions were half
depopulated, he summoned
to his presence a thousand
hale and light-hearted
friends from among the
knights and dames of
his court, and with these

retired to the deep seclusion of one of his castellated abbeys. This was an extensive and magnificent structure, the creation of the prince's own eccentric yet august taste. A strong and lofty wall girdled it in. This wall had gates of iron. The courtiers, having entered, brought furnaces and massy hammers and welded the bolts. They resolved to leave means neither of ingress nor egress to the sudden impulses of despair or of frenzy from within. The abbey was amply provisioned. With such precautions the courtiers might bid defiance to contagion. The external world could take care of itself. In the meantime it was folly to grieve, or to think. The prince had provided all the appliances of pleasure. There were buffoons, there were improvisatori, there were ballet–dancers, there were musicians, there was Beauty, there was wine. All these and security were within. Without was the "Red Death."

It was towards the close of the fifth or sixth month of his seclusion, and while the pestilence raged most furiously abroad, that the Prince Prospero entertained his thousand friends at a masked ball of the most unusual magnificence.

It was a voluptuous scene, that masquerade. But first let me tell of the rooms in which it was held. These were seven—an imperial suite. In many palaces, however, such suites form a long and straight vista, while the folding doors slide back nearly to the walls on either hand, so that the view of the whole extent is scarcely impeded. Here the case was very different, as might have been expected from the duke's love of the *bizarre*. The apartments were so irregularly disposed that the vision embraced but little more than one at a time. There was a sharp turn at every twenty or thirty yards, and at each turn a novel effect. To the right and left, in the middle of each wall, a tall and narrow Gothic window looked out upon a closed corridor which pursued the windings of the suite. These windows were of stained glass whose colour varied in accordance with the prevailing hue of the decorations of the chamber into which it opened. That at the eastern extremity was hung, for example, in blue—and vividly blue were its windows. The second chamber was purple in its ornaments and tapestries, and here the panes were purple. The third was green throughout, and so were the casements. The fourth was furnished and lighted with orange—the fifth with white—the sixth with violet. The seventh apartment was closely shrouded in black velvet tapestries that hung all over the ceiling and down the walls, falling in heavy folds upon a carpet of the same material and hue. But in this chamber only, the colour of the windows failed to correspond with the decorations. The panes here were scarlet—a deep blood colour. Now in no one of the seven apartments was there any lamp or candelabrum, amid the profusion of golden ornaments that lay scattered to and fro or depended from the roof. There was no light of any kind emanating from lamp or candle within the suite of chambers. But in the corridors that followed the suite, there stood, opposite to each window, a heavy tripod, bearing a brazier of fire, that projected its rays through the tinted glass and so glaringly illumined the room. And thus were produced a multitude of gaudy and fantastic appearances. But in the western or black chamber

the effect of the fire–light
that streamed upon the
dark hangings through the
blood–tinted panes was
ghastly in the extreme, and
produced so wild a look
upon the countenances
of those who entered,
that there were few of the
company bold enough to
set foot within its precincts
at all.

It was in this apartment,
also, that there stood
against the western wall,
a gigantic clock of ebony.
Its pendulum swung to
and fro with a dull, heavy,
monotonous clang; and
when the minute-hand
made the circuit of the face,
and the hour was to be
stricken, there came from
the brazen lungs of the

clock a sound which was
clear and loud and deep
and exceedingly musical,
but of so peculiar a note
and emphasis that, at
each lapse of an hour, the
musicians of the orchestra
were constrained to pause,
momentarily, in their
performance, to harken to
the sound; and thus the
waltzers perforce ceased

their evolutions; and there was a brief disconcert of the whole gay company; and, while the chimes of the clock yet rang, it was observed that the giddiest grew pale, and the more aged and sedate passed their hands over their brows as if in confused revery or meditation. But when the echoes had fully ceased, a light laughter at once pervaded the assembly; the musicians looked at each other and smiled as if at their own nervousness and folly, and made whispering vows, each to the other, that the next chiming of the clock should produce in them no similar emotion; and then, after the lapse of sixty minutes, (which embrace three thousand and six hundred seconds of the Time that flies,) there came yet another chiming of the clock, and then were the same disconcert and tremulousness and meditation as before.

But, in spite of these things, it was a gay and magnificent revel. The tastes of the duke were

peculiar. He had a fine eye
for colours and effects. He
disregarded the *decora* of
mere fashion. His plans
were bold and fiery, and
his conceptions glowed
with barbaric lustre. There
are some who would have
thought him mad. His fol-
lowers felt that he was not.
It was necessary to hear
and see and touch him to

be *sure* that he was not.

He had directed, in great part, the movable embellishments of the seven chambers, upon occasion of this great *fête*; and it was his own guiding taste which had given character to the masqueraders. Be sure they were grotesque. There were much glare and glitter and piquancy and phantasm—much of what has been since seen in "Her-nani." There were arabesque figures with unsuited limbs and appointments. There were delirious fancies such as the madman fashions. There were much of the beautiful, much of the wanton, much of the *bizarre*, something of the terrible, and not a little of that

which might have excited
disgust. To and fro in the
seven chambers there
stalked, in fact, a multitude
of dreams. And these—the
dreams—writhed in and
about, taking hue from the
rooms, and causing the
wild music of the orchestra
to seem as the echo of their
steps. And, anon, there
strikes the ebony clock

which stands in the hall of
the velvet. And then, for
a moment, all is still, and
all is silent save the voice
of the clock. The dreams
are stiff-frozen as they
stand. But the echoes of the
chime die away—they have
endured but an instant—
and a light, half-subdued
laughter floats after them
as they depart. And now

again the music swells, and the dreams live, and writhe to and fro more merrily than ever, taking hue from the many tinted windows through which stream the rays from the tripods. But to the chamber which lies most westwardly of the seven, there are now none of the maskers who venture; for the night is wan-ing away; and there flows a ruddier light through the blood-coloured panes; and the blackness of the sable drapery appals; and to him whose foot falls upon the sable carpet, there comes from the near clock of ebony a muffled peal more solemnly emphatic than any which reaches *their* ears who indulged in the more remote gaieties of the other apartments.

But these other apartments were densely crowded, and in them beat feverishly the heart of life. And the revel went whirlingly on, until at length there commenced the sounding of midnight upon the clock. And then the music ceased, as I have told; and the evolutions of the waltzers were quieted; and there was an uneasy cessation of all things as before. But now there were twelve strokes to be sounded by the bell of the clock; and thus it happened, perhaps, that more of thought crept, with more of time, into the meditations of the thoughtful among those who revelled. And thus too, it happened, perhaps, that before the last echoes of the last chime had utterly sunk into silence, there were many individuals in the crowd who had found leisure to become aware of the presence of a masked figure which had arrested the attention of no single individual before. And the rumour of this new presence having spread itself whisperingly around, there arose at length from the whole company a buzz, or murmur, expressive of disapprobation and surprise—then, finally, of terror, of horror, and of disgust.

In an assembly of phantasms such as I have

painted, it may well be supposed that no ordinary appearance could have excited such sensation. In truth the masquerade license of the night was nearly unlimited; but the figure in question had out-Heroded Herod, and gone beyond the bounds of even the prince's indefinite decorum. There are chords in the hearts of the most reckless which cannot be touched without emotion. Even with the utterly lost, to whom life and death are equally jests, there are matters of which no jest can be made. The whole company, indeed, seemed now deeply to feel that in the costume and bearing of the stranger neither wit nor propriety existed. The figure was tall and gaunt, and shrouded from head to foot in the habiliments of the grave. The mask which concealed the visage was made so nearly to resemble the countenance of a stiffened corpse that the closest scrutiny must have had difficulty in detecting the cheat. And yet all this

might have been endured,
if not approved, by the mad
revellers around. But the
mummer had gone so far
as to assume the type of
the Red Death. His vesture
was dabbled in *blood*—and
his broad brow, with all
the features of the face, was
besprinkled with the scarlet
horror.

When the eyes of the

Prince Prospero fell upon this spectral image (which, with a slow and solemn movement, as if more fully to sustain its role, stalked to and fro among the waltzers) he was seen to be convulsed, in the first moment with a strong shudder either of terror or distaste; but, in the next, his brow reddened with rage.

"Who dares,"—he demanded hoarsely of the courtiers who stood near him—"who dares insult us with this blasphemous mockery? Seize him and unmask him—that we may know whom we have to hang, at sunrise, from the battlements!"

It was in the eastern or blue chamber in which

stood the Prince Prospero as he uttered these words. They rang throughout the seven rooms loudly and clearly, for the prince was a bold and robust man, and the music had become hushed at the waving of his hand.

It was in the blue room where stood the prince, with a group of pale courtiers by his side. At first, as he spoke, there was a slight rushing movement of this group in the direction of the intruder, who at the moment was also near at hand, and now, with deliberate and stately step, made closer approach to the speaker. But from a certain nameless awe with which the mad assump–

tions of the mummer had
inspired the whole party,
there were found none
who put forth hand to seize
him; so that, unimpeded,
he passed within a yard of
the prince's person; and,
while the vast assembly,
as if with one impulse,
shrank from the centres
of the rooms to the walls,
he made his way uninter-

ruptedly, but with the same
solemn and measured step
which had distinguished
him from the first, through
the blue chamber to the
purple—through the purple
to the green—through
the green to the orange—
through this again to the
white—and even thence
to the violet, ere a decided
movement had been made

to arrest him. It was then, however, that the Prince Prospero, maddening with rage and the shame of his own momentary cowardice, rushed hurriedly through the six chambers, while none followed him on account of a deadly terror that had seized upon all. He bore aloft a drawn dagger, and had approached,

in rapid impetuosity, to
within three or four feet of
the retreating figure, when
the latter, having attained
the extremity of the velvet
apartment, turned suddenly
and confronted his pursuer.
There was a sharp cry—and
the dagger dropped gleam-
ing upon the sable carpet,
upon which, instantly
afterwards, fell prostrate

in death the Prince Pros-
pero. Then, summoning the
wild courage of despair, a
throng of the revellers at
once threw themselves into
the black apartment, and,
seizing the mummer, whose
tall figure stood erect and
motionless within the
shadow of the ebony clock,
gasped in unutterable
horror at finding the grave

cerements and corpse–like mask, which they handled with so violent a rudeness, untenanted by any tangible form.

And now was acknowledged the presence of the Red Death. He had come like a thief in the night. And one by one dropped the revellers in the blood–bedewed halls of their revel, and died each in the despairing posture of his fall. And the life of the ebony clock went out with that of the last of the gay. And the flames of the tripods expired. And Darkness and Decay and the Red Death held illimitable dominion over all.

THE
TELL–TALE
HEART

True!—nervous—very, very dreadfully nervous I had been and am; but why *will* you say that I am mad? The disease had sharpened my senses—not destroyed—not dulled them. Above all was the sense of hearing acute. I heard all things in the heaven and in the earth. I heard many things in hell. How, then, am I mad? Hearken! and observe how healthily— how calmly I can tell you the whole story.

It is impossible to say how first the idea entered my brain; but once con- ceived, it haunted me day and night. Object there was none. Passion there was none. I loved the old man. He had never wronged me. He had never given me insult. For his gold I had no desire. I think it was his eye! yes, it was this! He had the eye of a vulture—a pale blue eye, with a film over it. Whenever it fell upon me, my blood ran cold; and so

by degrees—very gradually—
I made up my mind to take
the life of the old man, and
thus rid myself of the eye
forever.

Now this is the point.
You fancy me mad. Mad-
men know nothing. But
you should have seen *me*.
You should have seen how
wisely I proceeded—with
what caution—with what

foresight—with what dis-
simulation I went to work! I
was never kinder to the old
man than during the whole
week before I killed him.
And every night, about
midnight, I turned the latch
of his door and opened
it—oh so gently! And then,
when I had made an open-
ing sufficient for my head,
I put in a dark lantern,

all closed, closed, that no light shone out, and then I thrust in my head. Oh, you would have laughed to see how cunningly I thrust it in! I moved it slowly—very, very slowly, so that I might not disturb the old man's sleep. It took me an hour to place my whole head within the opening so far that I could see him as

he lay upon his bed. Ha!
would a madman have
been so wise as this? And
then, when my head was
well in the room, I undid
the lantern cautiously—oh,
so cautiously—cautiously
(for the hinges creaked)—I
undid it just so much that
a single thin ray fell upon
the vulture eye. And this I
did for seven long nights—

every night just at mid-
night—but I found the eye
always closed; and so it was
impossible to do the work;
for it was not the old man
who vexed me, but his Evil
Eye. And every morning,
when the day broke, I went
boldly into the chamber,
and spoke courageously
to him, calling him by
name in a hearty tone,

and inquiring how he had passed the night. So you see he would have been a very profound old man, indeed, to suspect that every night, just at twelve, I looked in upon him while he slept.

Upon the eighth night I was more than usually cautious in opening the door. A watch's minute hand moves more quickly than did mine. Never before that night had I *felt* the extent of my own powers—of my sagacity. I could scarcely contain my feelings of triumph. To think that there I was, opening the door, little by little, and he not even to dream of my secret deeds or thoughts. I fairly chuckled at the idea;

and perhaps he heard me;
for he moved on the bed
suddenly, as if startled.
Now you may think that
I drew back—but no. His
room was as black as pitch
with the thick darkness,
(for the shutters were close
fastened, through fear of
robbers,) and so I knew
that he could not see the
opening of the door, and I

kept pushing it on steadily, steadily.

I had my head in, and was about to open the lantern, when my thumb slipped upon the tin fastening, and the old man sprang up in bed, crying out—"Who's there?"

I kept quite still and said nothing. For a whole hour I did not move a muscle, and in the meantime I did not hear him lie down. He was still sitting up in the bed listening;—just as I have done, night after night, hearkening to the death watches in the wall.

Presently I heard a slight groan, and I knew it was the groan of mortal terror. It was not a groan of pain or of grief—oh, no!—it was

the low stifled sound that
arises from the bottom of
the soul when overcharged
with awe. I knew the sound
well. Many a night, just
at midnight, when all the
world slept, it has welled
up from my own bosom,
deepening, with its dreadful echo, the terrors that
distracted me. I say I knew
it well. I knew what the

old man felt, and pitied
him, although I chuckled
at heart. I knew that he
had been lying awake ever
since the first slight noise,
when he had turned in the
bed. His fears had been
ever since growing upon
him. He had been trying to
fancy them causeless, but
could not. He had been
saying to himself—"It is

nothing but the wind in the chimney—it is only a mouse crossing the floor," or "it is merely a cricket which has made a single chirp." Yes, he had been trying to comfort himself with these suppositions: but he had found all in vain. *All in vain*; because Death, in approaching him, had stalked with his black shadow before him, and enveloped the victim. And it was the mournful influence of the unperceived shadow that caused him to feel—although he neither saw nor heard—to *feel* the presence of my head within the room.

When I had waited a long time, very patiently, without hearing him lie

down, I resolved to open
a little—a very, very little
crevice in the lantern.
So I opened it—you cannot
imagine how stealthily,
stealthily—until, at length
a simple dim ray, like the
thread of the spider, shot
from out the crevice and
fell full upon the vulture eye.

It was open—wide, wide
open—and I grew furious

as I gazed upon it. I saw
it with perfect distinct–
ness—all a dull blue, with
a hideous veil over it that
chilled the very marrow
in my bones; but I could
see nothing else of the old
man's face or person: for I
had directed the ray as if by
instinct, precisely upon the
damned spot.

And have I not told you

that what you mistake for
madness is but over-acute-
ness of the sense?—now, I
say, there came to my ears
a low, dull, quick sound,
such as a watch makes
when enveloped in cotton.
I knew *that* sound well,
too. It was the beating
of the old man's heart. It
increased my fury, as the
beating of a drum stimulates

the soldier into courage.

But even yet I refrained and kept still. I scarcely breathed. I held the lantern motionless. I tried how steadily I could main–tain the ray upon the eye. Meantime the hell–ish tattoo of the heart increased. It grew quicker and quicker, and louder and louder every instant.

The old man's terror *must* have been extreme! It grew louder, I say, louder every moment!—do you mark me well? I have told you that I am nervous: so I am. And now at the dead hour of the night, amid the dreadful silence of that old house, so strange a noise as this excited me to uncontrollable terror. Yet,

for some minutes lon-
ger I refrained and stood
still. But the beating grew
louder, louder! I thought
the heart must burst. And
now a new anxiety seized
me—the sound would be
heard by a neighbour!
The old man's hour had
come! With a loud yell, I
threw open the lantern and
leaped into the room. He

shrieked once—once only. In an instant I dragged him to the floor, and pulled the heavy bed over him. I then smiled gaily, to find the deed so far done. But, for many minutes, the heart beat on with a muffled sound. This, however, did not vex me; it would not be heard through the wall. At length it ceased. The old

man was dead. I removed
the bed and examined the
corpse. Yes, he was stone,
stone dead. I placed my
hand upon the heart and
held it there many minutes.
There was no pulsation.
He was stone dead. His eye
would trouble me no more.

If still you think me mad,
you will think so no longer
when I describe the wise

precautions I took for the concealment of the body. The night waned, and I worked hastily, but in silence. First of all I dismembered the corpse. I cut off the head and the arms and the legs.

I then took up three planks from the flooring of the chamber, and deposited all between the scantlings. I then replaced the boards so cleverly, so cunningly, that no human eye—not even *his*—could have detected anything wrong. There was nothing to wash out—no stain of any kind—no blood-spot whatever. I had been too wary for that. A tub had caught all—ha! ha!

When I had made an end of these labors, it was

four o'clock—still dark as midnight. As the bell sounded the hour, there came a knocking at the street door. I went down to open it with a light heart,— for what had I *now* to fear? There entered three men, who introduced them- selves, with perfect suavity, as officers of the police. A shriek had been heard by a neighbour during the night; suspicion of foul play had been aroused; information had been lodged at the police office, and they (the officers) had been deputed to search the premises.

I smiled,—for *what* had I to fear? I bade the gentlemen welcome. The shriek, I said, was my own in a dream. The old man,

I mentioned, was absent
in the country. I took my
visitors all over the house.
I bade them search—search
well. I led them, at length, to
his chamber. I showed them
his treasures, secure, undis-
turbed. In the enthusiasm
of my confidence, I brought
chairs into the room, and
desired them *here* to rest
from their fatigues, while I

myself, in the wild audac-
ity of my perfect triumph,
placed my own seat upon
the very spot beneath
which reposed the corpse
of the victim.

The officers were sat-
isfied. My *manner* had
convinced them. I was
singularly at ease. They
sat, and while I answered
cheerily, they chatted of

familiar things. But, ere long, I felt myself getting pale and wished them gone. My head ached, and I fancied a ringing in my ears: but still they sat and still chatted. The ringing became more distinct:—it continued and became more distinct: I talked more freely to get rid of the feeling: but it continued and gained definiteness—until, at length, I found that the noise was *not* within my ears.

No doubt I now grew *very* pale;—but I talked more fluently, and with a heightened voice. Yet the sound increased—and what could I do? It was *a low, dull, quick sound—much such a sound as a watch makes when enveloped in cotton.* I

gasped for breath—and yet
the officers heard it not.
I talked more quickly—
more vehemently; but the
noise steadily increased.
I arose and argued about
trifles, in a high key and
with violent gesticulations;
but the noise steadily
increased. Why *would*
they not be gone? I paced
the floor to and fro with

heavy strides, as if excited to fury by the observations of the men—but the noise steadily increased. Oh God! what *could* I do? I foamed—I raved—I swore! I swung the chair upon which I had been sitting, and grated it upon the boards, but the noise arose over all and continually increased. It grew

louder—louder—*louder*!
And still the men chatted
pleasantly, and smiled. Was
it possible they heard not?
Almighty God!—no, no!
They heard!—they sus-
pected!—they *knew*!—they
were making a mockery of
my horror!—this I thought,
and this I think. But anything was better than this
agony! Anything was more

tolerable than this derision! I
could bear those hypocritical
smiles no longer! I felt that
I must scream or die! and
now—again!—hark! louder!
louder! louder! *louder*!

"Villains!" I shrieked,
"dissemble no more! I
admit the deed!—tear up
the planks! here, here!—it is
the beating of his hideous
heart!"

THE CASK OF AMONTILLADO

The thousand inju-
ries of Fortunato I had
borne as I best could, but
when he ventured upon
insult I vowed revenge.
You, who so well know
the nature of my soul, will
not suppose, however,
that I gave utterance to a

threat. *At length* I would be avenged; this was a point definitely settled—but the very definitiveness with which it was resolved precluded the idea of risk. I must not only punish but punish with impunity. A wrong is unredressed when retribution overtakes its redresser. It is equally unredressed when the avenger fails to make himself felt as such to him who has done the wrong.

It must be understood that neither by word nor deed had I given Fortunato cause to doubt my good will. I continued, as was my wont, to smile in his face, and he did not perceive that my smile *now* was at the thought of his immolation.

He had a weak point—
this Fortunato—although in
other regards he was a man
to be respected and even
feared. He prided himself
on his connoisseurship in
wine. Few Italians have the
true virtuoso spirit. For the
most part their enthusiasm
is adopted to suit the time
and opportunity, to practise
imposture upon the British

and Austrian *millionaires*.
In painting and gemmary,
Fortunato, like his country-
men, was a quack, but in
the matter of old wines he
was sincere. In this respect
I did not differ from him
materially;—I was skilful in
the Italian vintages myself,
and bought largely when-
ever I could.

It was about dusk,

one evening during the supreme madness of the carnival season, that I encountered my friend. He accosted me with excessive warmth, for he had been drinking much. The man wore motley. He had on a tight-fitting parti-striped dress, and his head was surmounted by the conical cap and bells. I was so pleased to see him that I thought I should never have done wringing his hand.

I said to him—"My dear Fortunato, you are luckily met. How remarkably well you are looking today. But I have received a pipe of what passes for Amon-tillado, and I have my doubts."

"How?" said he. "Amontillado? A pipe? Impossible! And in the middle of the carnival!"

"I have my doubts," I replied; "and I was silly enough to pay the full Amontillado price without consulting you in the matter. You were not to be found, and I was fearful of losing a bargain."

"Amontillado!"

"I have my doubts."

"Amontillado!"

"And I must satisfy them."

"Amontillado!"

"As you are engaged, I am on my way to Luchresi. If anyone has a critical turn it is he. He will tell me—"

"Luchresi cannot tell Amontillado from Sherry."

"And yet some fools will

have it that his taste is a
match for your own."

"Come, let us go."

"Whither?"

"To your vaults."

"My friend, no; I will not
impose upon your good
nature. I perceive you have
an engagement. Luchresi—"

"I have no engagement;—
come."

"My friend, no. It is not

the engagement, but the severe cold with which I perceive you are afflicted. The vaults are insufferably damp. They are encrusted with nitre."

"Let us go, nevertheless. The cold is merely nothing. Amontillado! You have been imposed upon. And as for Luchresi, he cannot distinguish Sherry from Amontillado."

Thus speaking, Fortunato possessed himself of my arm; and putting on a mask of black silk and drawing a *roquelaire* closely about my person, I suffered him to hurry me to my palazzo.

There were no attendants at home; they had absconded to make merry in honour of the time. I had told them that I should not return until the morning, and had given them explicit orders not to stir from the house. These orders were sufficient, I well knew, to insure their immediate disappearance, one and all, as soon as my back was turned.

I took from their sconces two flambeaux, and giving one to Fortunato, bowed him through several suites of rooms to the archway that led into the vaults. I passed down a long and winding staircase, requesting him to be cautious as he followed. We came at length to the foot of the descent, and stood together upon the damp ground of the catacombs of the Montresors.

The gait of my friend was

unsteady, and the bells upon his cap jingled as he strode.

"The pipe," said he.

"It is farther on," said I; "but observe the white web-work which gleams from these cavern walls."

He turned towards me, and looked into my eyes with two filmy orbs that distilled the rheum of intoxication.

"Nitre?" he asked, at length.

"Nitre," I replied. "How long have you had that cough?"

"Ugh! ugh! ugh!—ugh! ugh! ugh!—ugh! ugh! ugh!—ugh! ugh! ugh!—ugh! ugh! ugh!"

My poor friend found it impossible to reply for many minutes.

"It is nothing" he said, at last.

"Come," I said, with decision, "we will go back; your health is precious. You are rich, respected, admired, beloved; you are happy, as once I was. You are a man to be missed. For me it is no matter. We will go back; you will be ill, and I cannot be responsible. Besides, there is Luchresi—"

"Enough," he said; "the cough is a mere nothing; it will not kill me. I shall not die of a cough."

"True—true," I replied; "and, indeed, I had no intention of alarming you unnecessarily—but you should use all proper caution. A draught of this Medoc will defend us from the damps."

Here I knocked off the neck of a bottle which I drew from a long row of its fellows that lay upon the mould.

"Drink," I said, presenting him the wine.

He raised it to his lips with a leer. He paused and nodded to me familiarly, while his bells jingled.

"I drink," he said, "to the

buried that repose around us."

"And I to your long life."

He again took my arm, and we proceeded.

"These vaults," he said, "are extensive."

"The Montresors," I replied, "were a great and numerous family."

"I forget your arms."

"A huge human foot d'or,

in a field azure; the foot
crushes a serpent rampant
whose fangs are imbedded
in the heel."

"And the motto?"

"Nemo me impune lacessit."

"Good!" he said.

The wine sparkled in his
eyes and the bells jingled.
My own fancy grew warm
with the Medoc. We had
passed through long walls

of piled skeletons, with casks and puncheons inter-mingling, into the inmost recesses of catacombs. I paused again, and this time I made bold to seize Fortunato by an arm above the elbow.

"The nitre!" I said; "see, it increases. It hangs like moss upon the vaults. We are below the river's bed.

The drops of moisture trickle among the bones. Come, we will go back ere it is too late. Your cough—"

"It is nothing," he said; "let us go on. But first, another draught of the Medoc."

I broke and reached him a flagon of De Grâve. He emptied it at a breath. His eyes flashed with a fierce

light. He laughed and threw
the bottle upwards with
a gesticulation I did not
understand.

I looked at him in surprise.
He repeated the move-
ment—a grotesque one.

"You do not compre-
hend?" he said.

"Not I," I replied.

"Then you are not of the
brotherhood."

"How?"

"You are not of the masons."

"Yes, yes," I said; "yes, yes."

"You? Impossible! A mason?"

"A mason," I replied.

"A sign," he said, "a sign."

"It is this," I answered, producing from beneath the folds of my *roquelaire* a trowel.

"You jest," he exclaimed, recoiling a few paces. "But let us proceed to the Amontillado."

"Be it so," I said, replacing the tool beneath the cloak and again offering him my arm. He leaned upon it heavily. We continued our route in search of the Amontillado. We passed through a range of low arches, descended, passed on, and descending again, arrived at a deep crypt, in which the foulness of the air caused our flambeaux rather to glow than flame.

At the most remote end of the crypt there appeared another less spacious. Its walls had been lined with human remains, piled to the vault overhead, in the fashion of the great catacombs of Paris. Three sides of this interior crypt were still ornamented in this manner. From the fourth side the bones had been thrown down, and lay promiscuously upon the earth, forming at one point a mound of some size. Within the wall thus exposed by the displacing

of the bones, we per–
ceived a still interior crypt
or recess, in depth about
four feet, in width three,
in height six or seven.
It seemed to have been
constructed for no espe-
cial use within itself, but
formed merely the interval
between two of the colossal
supports of the roof of the
catacombs, and was backed

by one of their circumscrib-
ing walls of solid granite.

It was in vain that Fortunato, uplifting his dull torch,
endeavoured to pry into
the depth of the recess. Its
termination the feeble light
did not enable us to see.

"Proceed," I said; "herein
is the Amontillado. As for
Luchresi—"

"He is an ignoramus,"

interrupted my friend,
as he stepped unsteadily
forward, while I followed
immediately at his heels. In
an instant he had reached
the extremity of the niche,
and finding his progress
arrested by the rock, stood
stupidly bewildered. A
moment more and I had
fettered him to the granite.
In its surface were two iron

staples, distant from each other about two feet, horizontally. From one of these depended a short chain, from the other a padlock. Throwing the links about his waist, it was but the work of a few seconds to secure it. He was too much astounded to resist. Withdrawing the key I stepped back from the recess.

"Pass your hand," I said, "over the wall; you can—not help feeling the nitre. Indeed, it is *very* damp. Once more let me *implore* you to return. No? Then I must positively leave you. But I must first render you all the little attentions in my power."

"The Amontillado!" ejaculated my friend, not yet

recovered from his astonishment.

"True," I replied; "the Amontillado."

As I said these words I busied myself among the pile of bones of which I have before spoken. Throwing them aside, I soon uncovered a quantity of building stone and mortar. With these materials and with the aid of my trowel, I began vigorously to wall up the entrance of the niche.

I had scarcely laid the first tier of the masonry when I discovered that the intoxication of Fortunato had in a great measure worn off. The earliest indication I had of this was a low moaning cry from the depth of the recess. It was *not* the cry of a drunken man. There was then a long and obstinate silence. I laid the second tier, and the third, and the fourth; and then I heard the furious vibrations of the chain. The noise lasted for several minutes, during which, that I might hearken to it with the more satisfaction,

I ceased my labours and sat down upon the bones. When at last the clanking subsided, I resumed the trowel, and finished without interruption the fifth, the sixth, and the seventh tier. The wall was now nearly upon a level with my breast. I again paused, and holding the flambeaux over the mason-work,

threw a few feeble rays
upon the figure within.

A succession of loud and
shrill screams, bursting
suddenly from the throat of
the chained form, seemed
to thrust me violently
back. For a brief moment
I hesitated—I trembled.
Unsheathing my rapier,
I began to grope with it
about the recess; but the

thought of an instant reas-
sured me. I placed my hand
upon the solid fabric of the
catacombs, and felt satisfied. I re-approached the
wall; I replied to the yells
of him who clamoured. I
re-echoed, I aided, I sur-
passed them in volume and
in strength. I did this, and
the clamourer grew still.

It was now midnight, and

my task was drawing to a close. I had completed the eighth, the ninth, and the tenth tier. I had finished a portion of the last and the eleventh; there remained but a single stone to be fitted and plastered in. I struggled with its weight; I placed it partially in its destined position. But now there came from out the

niche a low laugh that
erected the hairs upon my
head. It was succeeded by
a sad voice, which I had
difficulty in recognizing as
that of the noble Fortunato.
The voice said—

"Ha! ha! ha!—he! he!
he!—a very good joke,
indeed—an excellent jest.
We will have many a rich
laugh about it at the pala-

zzo—he! he! he!—over our wine—he! he! he!"

"The Amontillado!" I said.

"He! he! he!—he! he! he!—yes, the Amontillado. But is it not getting late? Will not they be awaiting us at the palazzo, the Lady Fortunato and the rest? Let us be gone."

"Yes," I said, "let us be gone."

"For the love of God, Montresor!"

"Yes," I said, "for the love of God!"

But to these words I hearkened in vain for a reply. I grew impatient. I called aloud—

"Fortunato!"

No answer. I called again—

"Fortunato!"

No answer still. I thrust a torch through the remaining aperture and let it fall within. There came forth in return only a jingling of the bells. My heart grew sick; it was the dampness of the catacombs that made it so. I hastened to make an end of my labour. I forced the last stone into its position; I plastered it up. Against the

new masonry I re-erected
the old rampart of bones.
For the half of a century no
mortal has disturbed them.
In pace requiescat!

THE
BLACK CAT

For the most wild, yet most homely nar–rative which I am about to pen, I neither expect nor solicit belief. Mad indeed would I be to expect it, in a case where my very senses reject their own evidence. Yet, mad am I

not—and very surely do I not dream. But to-morrow I die, and to-day I would unburthen my soul. My immediate purpose is to place before the world, plainly, succinctly, and without comment, a series of mere household events. In their consequences, these events have terri-fied—have tortured—have

destroyed me. Yet I will not
attempt to expound them.
To me, they have presented
little but Horror—to many
they will seem less terrible
than *baroques*. Hereafter,
perhaps, some intellect may
be found which will reduce
my phantasm to the com-
mon-place—some intellect
more calm, more logical,
and far less excitable than

my own, which will per-
ceive, in the circumstances
I detail with awe, nothing
more than an ordinary
succession of very natural
causes and effects.

From my infancy I was
noted for the docility and
humanity of my dispo-
sition. My tenderness of
heart was even so conspic-
uous as to make me the jest

of my companions. I was especially fond of animals, and was indulged by my parents with a great variety of pets. With these I spent most of my time, and never was so happy as when feeding and caressing them. This peculiarity of character grew with my growth, and, in my manhood, I derived from it one of my princi–

pal sources of pleasure. To those who have cherished an affection for a faithful and sagacious dog, I need hardly be at the trouble of explaining the nature or the intensity of the gratification thus derivable. There is something in the unselfish and self-sacrificing love of a brute, which goes directly to the heart of him who has had frequent occasion to test the paltry friendship and gossamer fidelity of mere *Man*.

I married early, and was happy to find in my wife a disposition not uncongenial with my own. Observing my partiality for domestic pets, she lost no opportunity of procuring those of the most agreeable kind.

We had birds, gold fish, a fine dog, rabbits, a small monkey, and *a cat*.

This latter was a remarkably large and beautiful animal, entirely black, and sagacious to an astonishing degree. In speaking of his intelligence, my wife, who at heart was not a little tinctured with superstition, made frequent allusion to

the ancient popular notion,
which regarded all black
cats as witches in disguise.
Not that she was ever *serious* upon this point—and
I mention the matter at all
for no better reason than
that it happens, just now, to
be remembered.

Pluto—this was the cat's
name—was my favourite
pet and playmate. I alone

fed him, and he attended
me wherever I went about
the house. It was even
with difficulty that I could
prevent him from following
me through the streets.

Our friendship lasted,
in this manner, for several
years, during which my
general temperament and
character—through the
instrumentality of the Fiend

Intemperance—had (I blush to confess it) experienced a radical alteration for the worse. I grew, day by day, more moody, more irritable, more regardless of the feelings of others. I suffered myself to use intemperate language to my wife. At length, I even offered her personal violence. My pets, of course, were

made to feel the change
in my disposition. I not
only neglected, but ill-used
them. For Pluto, however,
I still retained sufficient
regard to restrain me from
maltreating him, as I made
no scruple of maltreating
the rabbits, the monkey,
or even the dog, when
by accident, or through
affection, they came in my

way. But my disease grew upon me—for what disease is like Alcohol!—and at length even Pluto, who was now becoming old, and consequently somewhat peevish—even Pluto began to experience the effects of my ill temper.

One night, returning home, much intoxicated, from one of my haunts

about town, I fancied that
the cat avoided my pres-
ence. I seized him; when,
in his fright at my violence,
he inflicted a slight wound
upon my hand with his
teeth. The fury of a demon
instantly possessed me.
I knew myself no longer.
My original soul seemed,
at once, to take its flight
from my body; and a more

than fiendish malevolence,
gin-nurtured, thrilled every
fibre of my frame. I took
from my waistcoat-pocket
a pen-knife, opened it,
grasped the poor beast by
the throat, and deliberately
cut one of its eyes from
the socket! I blush, I burn,
I shudder, while I pen the
damnable atrocity.

When reason returned

with the morning—when
I had slept off the fumes
of the night's debauch—I
experienced a sentiment
half of horror, half of
remorse, for the crime of
which I had been guilty;
but it was, at best, a feeble
and equivocal feeling,
and the soul remained
untouched. I again plunged
into excess, and soon

drowned in wine all mem-
ory of the deed.

In the meantime the
cat slowly recovered. The
socket of the lost eye presented, it is true, a frightful
appearance, but he no
longer appeared to suffer
any pain. He went about
the house as usual, but,
as might be expected, fled
in extreme terror at my

approach. I had so much of my old heart left, as to be at first grieved by this evident dislike on the part of a creature which had once so loved me. But this feeling soon gave place to irritation. And then came, as if to my final and irrevocable overthrow, the spirit of PERVERSENESS. Of this spirit philosophy takes no

account. Yet I am not more
sure that my soul lives,
than I am that perverse-
ness is one of the primitive
impulses of the human
heart—one of the indi-
visible primary faculties,
or sentiments, which give
direction to the character
of Man. Who has not, a
hundred times, found him-
self committing a vile or

a silly action, for no other
reason than because he
knows he should *not*? Have
we not a perpetual incli-
nation, in the teeth of our
best judgment, to violate
that which is *Law*, merely
because we understand it
to be such? This spirit of
perverseness, I say, came to
my final overthrow. It was
this unfathomable longing

of the soul to *vex itself*—to offer violence to its own nature—to do wrong for the wrong's sake only—that urged me to continue and finally to consummate the injury I had inflicted upon the unoffending brute. One morning, in cool blood, I slipped a noose about its neck and hung it to the limb of a tree;—hung it

with the tears streaming
from my eyes, and with
the bitterest remorse at
my heart;—hung it *because*
I knew that it had loved
me, and *because* I felt it had
given me no reason of
offence;—hung it *because*
I knew that in so doing I
was committing a sin—a
deadly sin that would so
jeopardize my immortal

soul as to place it—if such a thing wore possible—even beyond the reach of the infinite mercy of the Most Merciful and Most Terrible God.

On the night of the day on which this cruel deed was done, I was aroused from sleep by the cry of fire. The curtains of my bed were in flames. The whole house was blazing. It was with great difficulty that my wife, a servant, and myself, made our escape from the conflagration. The destruction was complete. My entire worldly wealth was swallowed up, and I resigned myself thenceforward to despair.

I am above the weakness of seeking to establish

a sequence of cause and
effect, between the disaster
and the atrocity. But I am
detailing a chain of facts—
and wish not to leave even
a possible link imperfect.
On the day succeeding
the fire, I visited the ruins.
The walls, with one exception, had fallen in. This
exception was found in a
compartment wall, not very

thick, which stood about the middle of the house, and against which had rested the head of my bed. The plastering had here, in great measure, resisted the action of the fire—a fact which I attributed to its having been recently spread. About this wall a dense crowd were collected, and many persons seemed to be examining a particular portion of it with very minute and eager attention. The words "strange!" "singular!" and other similar expressions, excited my curiosity. I approached and saw, as if graven in *bas relief* upon the white surface, the figure of a gigantic *cat*. The impression was given with an accuracy truly mar–

vellous. There was a rope about the animal's neck.

When I first beheld this apparition—for I could scarcely regard it as less—my wonder and my terror were extreme. But at length reflection came to my aid. The cat, I remembered, had been hung in a garden adjacent to the house. Upon the alarm of fire, this

garden had been immedi-
ately filled by the crowd—
by someone of whom the
animal must have been cut
from the tree and thrown,
through an open window,
into my chamber. This had
probably been done with
the view of arousing me
from sleep. The falling of
other walls had compressed
the victim of my cruelty

into the substance of the freshly-spread plaster; the lime of which, with the flames, and the *ammonia* from the carcass, had then accomplished the portraiture as I saw it.

Although I thus readily accounted to my reason, if not altogether to my conscience, for the startling fact just detailed, it did not

the less fail to make a deep
impression upon my fancy.
For months I could not rid
myself of the phantasm of
the cat; and, during this
period, there came back
into my spirit a half–sentiment that seemed, but was
not, remorse. I went so far
as to regret the loss of the
animal, and to look about
me, among the vile haunts

which I now habitually frequented, for another pet of the same species, and of somewhat similar appearance, with which to supply its place.

One night as I sat, half stupified, in a den of more than infamy, my attention was suddenly drawn to some black object, reposing upon the head of one

of the immense hogsheads
of Gin, or of Rum, which
constituted the chief fur-
niture of the apartment. I
had been looking steadily
at the top of this hogshead
for some minutes, and what
now caused me surprise
was the fact that I had not
sooner perceived the object
thereupon. I approached
it, and touched it with my

hand. It was a black cat—a very large one—fully as large as Pluto, and closely resembling him in every respect but one. Pluto had not a white hair upon any portion of his body; but this cat had a large, although indefinite splotch of white, covering nearly the whole region of the breast. Upon my touching him, he immediately arose, purred loudly, rubbed against my hand, and appeared delighted with my notice. This, then, was the very creature of which I was in search. I at once offered to purchase it of the landlord; but this person made no claim to it—knew nothing of it—had never seen it before.

I continued my caresses,

and, when I prepared to go home, the animal evinced a disposition to accompany me. I permitted it to do so; occasionally stooping and patting it as I proceeded. When it reached the house it domesticated itself at once, and became immediately a great favorite with my wife.

For my own part, I soon

found a dislike to it arising
within me. This was just the
reverse of what I had antic-
ipated; but I know not how
or why it was—its evident
fondness for myself rather
disgusted and annoyed. By
slow degrees, these feelings
of disgust and annoyance
rose into the bitterness
of hatred. I avoided the
creature; a certain sense

of shame, and the remem-
brance of my former deed
of cruelty, preventing me
from physically abusing it.
I did not, for some weeks,
strike, or otherwise vio-
lently ill use it; but gradually—very gradually—I
came to look upon it with
unutterable loathing, and
to flee silently from its odi-
ous presence, as from the

breath of a pestilence.

What added, no doubt, to my hatred of the beast, was the discovery, on the morning after I brought it home, that, like Pluto, it also had been deprived of one of its eyes. This circumstance, however, only endeared it to my wife, who, as I have already said, possessed, in a high degree, that humanity of feeling which had once been my distinguishing trait, and the source of many of my simplest and purest pleasures.

With my aversion to this cat, however, its partial- ity for myself seemed to increase. It followed my footsteps with a pertinacity which it would be difficult to make the reader com–

prehend. Whenever I sat, it would crouch beneath my chair, or spring upon my knees, covering me with its loathsome caresses. If I arose to walk it would get between my feet and thus nearly throw me down, or, fastening its long and sharp claws in my dress, clamber, in this manner, to my breast. At such times, although I longed to destroy it with a blow, I was yet withheld from so doing, partly by a memory of my former crime, but chiefly—let me confess it at once—by absolute *dread* of the beast.

This dread was not exactly a dread of physical evil—and yet I should be at a loss how otherwise

to define it. I am almost
ashamed to own—yes,
even in this felon's cell,
I am almost ashamed to
own—that the terror and
horror with which the
animal inspired me, had
been heightened by one
of the merest chimæras it
would be possible to con-
ceive. My wife had called
my attention, more than

once, to the character of the mark of white hair, of which I have spoken, and which constituted the sole visible difference between the strange beast and the one I had destroyed. The reader will remember that this mark, although large, had been originally very indefinite; but, by slow degrees—degrees nearly imperceptible, and which for a long time my reason struggled to reject as fanciful—it had, at length, assumed a rigorous distinctness of outline. It was now the representation of an object that I shudder to name—and for this, above all, I loathed, and dreaded, and would have rid myself of the monster *had I dared*—

it was now, I say, the image of a hideous—of a ghastly thing—of the GALLOWS!— oh, mournful and terrible engine of Horror and of Crime—of Agony and of Death!

And now was I indeed wretched beyond the wretchedness of mere Humanity. And *a brute beast*—whose fellow I had contemptuously destroyed—*a brute beast* to work out for *me*—for me a man, fashioned in the image of the High God—so much of insufferable woe! Alas! neither by day nor by night knew I the blessing of Rest anymore! During the former the creature left me no moment alone; and, in the latter, I started, hourly,

from dreams of unutterable
fear, to find the hot breath
of *the thing* upon my face,
and its vast weight—an
incarnate Night–Mare that
I had no power to shake
off—incumbent eternally
upon my *heart!*

Beneath the pressure of
torments such as these, the
feeble remnant of the good
within me succumbed.

Evil thoughts became my
sole intimates—the darkest
and most evil of thoughts.
The moodiness of my
usual temper increased to
hatred of all things and of
all mankind; while, from
the sudden, frequent, and
ungovernable outbursts
of a fury to which I now
blindly abandoned myself,
my uncomplaining wife,

alas! was the most usual and the most patient of sufferers.

One day she accompanied me, upon some household errand, into the cellar of the old building which our poverty compelled us to inhabit. The cat followed me down the steep stairs, and, nearly throwing me headlong,

exasperated me to mad-
ness. Uplifting an axe, and
forgetting, in my wrath, the
childish dread which had
hitherto stayed my hand, I
aimed a blow at the animal
which, of course, would
have proved instantly
fatal had it descended as I
wished. But this blow was
arrested by the hand of
my wife. Goaded, by the

interference, into a rage more than demoniacal, I withdrew my arm from her grasp and buried the axe in her brain. She fell dead upon the spot, without a groan.

This hideous murder accomplished, I set myself forthwith, and with entire deliberation, to the task of concealing the body.

I knew that I could not
remove it from the house,
either by day or by night,
without the risk of being
observed by the neighbors.
Many projects entered
my mind. At one period
I thought of cutting the
corpse into minute frag-
ments, and destroying
them by fire. At another, I
resolved to dig a grave for

it in the floor of the cellar. Again, I deliberated about casting it in the well in the yard—about packing it in a box, as if merchandize, with the usual arrangements, and so getting a porter to take it from the house. Finally I hit upon what I considered a far better expedient than either of these. I determined to wall it up in the cellar—as the monks of the middle ages are recorded to have walled up their victims.

For a purpose such as this the cellar was well adapted. Its walls were loosely constructed, and had lately been plastered throughout with a rough plaster, which the dampness of the atmosphere had prevented from hardening. Moreover, in one of the walls was a projection, caused by a false chimney, or fireplace, that had been filled up, and made to resemble the rest of the cellar. I made no doubt that I could readily displace the bricks at this point, insert the corpse, and wall the whole up as before, so that

no eye could detect any-
thing suspicious.

And in this calculation
I was not deceived. By
means of a crowbar I easily
dislodged the bricks, and,
having carefully deposited
the body against the inner
wall, I propped it in that
position, while, with little
trouble, I re-laid the whole
structure as it originally

stood. Having procured mortar, sand, and hair, with every possible precaution, I prepared a plaster which could not be distinguished from the old, and with this I very carefully went over the new brick-work. When I had finished, I felt satisfied that all was right. The wall did not present the slightest appearance of having been disturbed. The rubbish on the floor was picked up with the minutest care. I looked around triumphantly, and said to myself—"Here at least, then, my labor has not been in vain."

My next step was to look for the beast which had been the cause of so much wretchedness; for I had, at length, firmly resolved to put it to death. Had I been able to meet with it, at the moment, there could have been no doubt of its fate; but it appeared that the crafty animal had been alarmed at the violence of my previous anger, and forebore to present itself in my present mood. It is impossible to describe, or to imagine, the deep, the blissful sense of relief which the absence of the detested creature occasioned in my bosom. It did not make its appearance during the night—and thus for one night at least, since its introduction into the house, I soundly and tranquilly slept; aye, *slept* even with the burden of murder upon my soul!

The second and the third day passed, and still my tormentor came not. Once again I breathed as a free-man. The monster, in terror, had fled the premises for-ever! I should behold it no more! My happiness was supreme! The guilt of my dark deed disturbed me but little. Some few inquiries had been made, but these had been readily answered. Even a search had been instituted—but of course nothing was to be discovered. I looked upon my future felicity as secured.

Upon the fourth day of the assassination, a party of the police came, very unexpectedly, into the house, and proceeded again to make rigorous investigation of the premises. Secure, however, in the inscrutability of my place of concealment, I felt no embarrassment whatever. The officers bade me accompany them in their search. They left no nook or corner unexplored. At length, for the third or fourth time, they descended

into the cellar. I quivered
not in a muscle. My heart
beat calmly as that of one
who slumbers in innocence.
I walked the cellar from
end to end. I folded my
arms upon my bosom, and
roamed easily to and fro.
The police were thoroughly
satisfied and prepared to
depart. The glee at my
heart was too strong to be

restrained. I burned to say
if but one word, by way
of triumph, and to render
doubly sure their assurance
of my guiltlessness.

"Gentlemen," I said at
last, as the party ascended
the steps, "I delight to have
allayed your suspicions. I
wish you all health, and
a little more courtesy.
By the bye, gentlemen,

this—this is a very well constructed house." [In the rabid desire to say something easily, I scarcely knew what I uttered at all.]—"I may say an *excellently* well constructed house. These walls—are you going, gentlemen?—these walls are solidly put together;" and here, through the mere phrenzy of bravado, I

rapped heavily, with a cane
which I held in my hand,
upon that very portion
of the brick-work behind
which stood the corpse of
the wife of my bosom.

But may God shield
and deliver me from the
fangs of the Arch-Fiend!
No sooner had the rever-
beration of my blows sunk
into silence, than I was

answered by a voice from
within the tomb!—by a cry,
at first muffled and broken,
like the sobbing of a child,
and then quickly swelling
into one long, loud, and
continuous scream, utterly
anomalous and inhu—
man—a howl—a wailing
shriek, half of horror and
half of triumph, such as
might have arisen only

out of hell, conjointly from the throats of the dammed in their agony and of the demons that exult in the damnation.

Of my own thoughts it is folly to speak. Swooning, I staggered to the opposite wall. For one instant the party upon the stairs remained motionless, through extremity of terror

and of awe. In the next, a
dozen stout arms were toil-
ing at the wall. It fell bodily.
The corpse, already greatly
decayed and clotted with
gore, stood erect before the
eyes of the spectators. Upon
its head, with red extended
mouth and solitary eye of
fire, sat the hideous beast
whose craft had seduced
me into murder, and whose

informing voice had con-
signed me to the hangman.
I had walled the monster
up within the tomb!

ART CREDITS

This book has been bound using handcraft methods and Smyth-sewn to ensure durability.

Designed by
Amanda Richmond.

Written and compiled by
T.L. Bonaddio.

Edited by Jennifer Leczkowski.

The text was set in Nofret.